3 - 02

19X
4/11

CR

D0398292

JERDINE NOLEN

Max and Jax
in Second Grade

Illustrated by
Karen Lee Schmidt

SILVER WHISTLE
HARCOURT, INC.
San Diego   New York   London

Requests for permission to make copies of any part
of the work should be mailed to the following address:
Permissions Department, Harcourt, Inc.,
6277 Sea Harbor Drive, Orlando, Florida 32887-6777.

www.harcourt.com

Silver Whistle is a trademark of Harcourt, Inc.,
registered in the United States of America and/or other jurisductions.

Library of Congress Cataloging-in-Publication Data
Nolen, Jerdine.
Max and Jax in second grade/by Jerdine Nolen;
illustrated by Karen Lee Schmidt.
p. cm.—(An Easy Reader Series)
Summary: Second grade twins Max and Jax prepare to start
the summer off right with a fishing trip and a slumber party.
[1. Twins—Fiction. 2. Brothers and sisters—Fiction.]
I. Schmidt, Karen, ill. II. Title. III. Series.
PZ7.N723Max 2002
[E]—dc21   98-5544
ISBN 0-15-201668-6

First edition
A C E G H F D B
Manufactured in China

The illustrations in this book were done in Windsor Newton watercolors
on Arches cold-pressed watercolor paper.
The display type was set in Giovanni Bold.
The text type was set in Giovanni Book.
Color separations by Colourscan Co. Pte. Ltd., Singapore
Manufactured by South China Printing Company, China
This book was printed on totally chlorine-free Nymolla Matte Art paper.
Production supervision by Sandra Grebenar and Pascha Gerlinger
Designed by Linda Lockowitz

To Matthew and Jessica, for luck

—J. N.

33

17

4

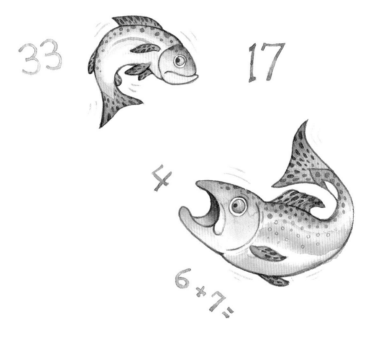

6 + 7 =

Contents

1
Fishing Dreams

Max thought about fishing
all the time.

Sometimes he wished he could
go fishing instead of going to school.
He even dreamed about fishing.

His twin sister, Jax, liked fishing, too.
But not as much.
She always caught lots of fish.
Max thought she was lucky.
Jax knew it was her special bait.

On Monday, Max ran up the stairs
carrying a small box.
Jax carried the rest of the mail.
"It came! It came!" Max called.
"What came?" asked Mom.
"My new fishing lure," Max said.
"Just in time for our fishing trip."

He opened the box.
Green and orange feathers
were attached to a string.
"Very nice," Jax said.
Max wanted to catch lots of fish—
at least as many as Jax had caught last time.
After all, the box said,
GUARANTEED TO WORK.

2
Max

The very first thing on Tuesday,
Max had journal writing.
He printed on his paper:
   A Perfect Way to Begin
   Summer Vacation.
He wrote about his weekend plans.
   Dad and I are going to camp out,
   sleep in a tent under the stars,
   and catch lots of big fish.
   I just got my new fishing lure.
   It is guaranteed to work.
He wrote on and on.
He filled up both sides of his paper.
His hand was not even tired.
It was time to stop.
There were other things to do.

7

Max had a hard time during spelling.
During math, the numbers
moved around on the page.
It was hard to add them.
It was harder to subtract them.
Most of his answers were wrong.
All Max could think about
was summer vacation.
It was just three days away.
Then—no school,
no homework,
no worries.
Just lots and lots of fish!

3
Jax

On Wednesday, Jax was working on a list.
Who would come to her sleep-over?
She looked at the blank paper.
She wrote:
    Marie,
    Tara,
    Katie,
    Rosie,
    Bonnie.
Her summer vacation would start
just as it should.

Then Jax made another list:
    Reasons to Be Glad
    Second Grade Is Over
She drew two lines
under the title
with her lucky colors,
green and purple.
At the very top
of her list she wrote:
    Third Grade

Then she wrote:
    Run for class president
Next she wrote:
    Use markers in art class
    Ride my bike to school
    Be one of the Big Kids
    Lunch at 12:00
    Office helper
    Kindergarten helper
    The talent show!!!!
    Good-bye, second grade!
    Third grade, here I come!
    When she finished,
there were eleven things on her list.

4
Lucky Bait

Finally, it was Friday.
Ring. Ring.
"School is out!" Mrs. Peters said.
"Have a great summer vacation."
Jax was with her friends
on the playground.
They were making more
sleep-over plans.

Later, at home, the doorbell rang
and rang,
and rang,
and rang,
and rang.

Each time the doorbell rang,
Max groaned.
That night, Max put a sign
on his bedroom door.
It read: DO NOT ENTER—THIS MEANS YOU!!!

Max went to the kitchen
one more time
to check his supplies.
Jax was mixing some things in a bowl.
"What are you doing?" Max asked.
"Making bait for you, of course," Jax said.

"Your special bait?" Max asked.

"My Secret Lucky Fishing Bait," Jax replied.

"For me?" Max asked.

"For luck," Jax said.

"It never fails."

19

5
A Good Alarm Clock

It was hard to sleep.
Max turned over.
He opened his eyes.
He looked at the clock.
He counted some of the seconds.
He listened for laughter.
But everything in the house was quiet.

Max went back to sleep.
Jake yawned and nuzzled closer.
Max patted Jake's head.
At five o'clock, Max woke up.
"Good morning, Jake," Max said,
scratching Jake's chin.

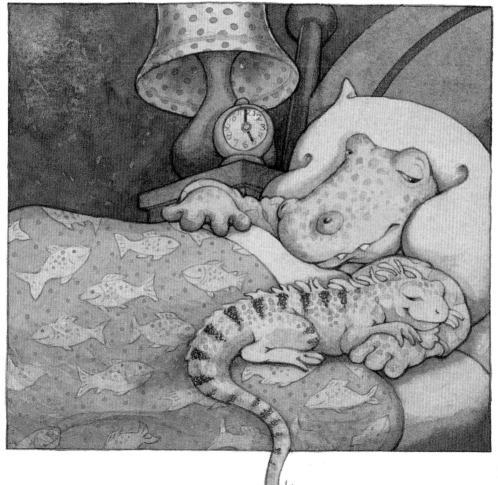

"Wake up, Dad. Time to go fishing!"
Max begged, "Let's go now!"
"Shhhh," Mom said sleepily.

6
Gone Fishing

Early on Saturday,
Max and Dad went fishing.
They rented a small boat
and rowed out to
the middle of the lake.
"This is going to be just great!" Max said.
"You are right," Dad replied.
"No worries, no problems—
just each other and the fish
we are going to catch!"
The sun was coming up.
Max's life jacket felt snug but nice.
He was glad he had his hat.
"Let's see the new fishing lure," Dad said.
"It's a beauty."

"And, it is guaranteed to work!"
Max replied.
Max looked at Jax's special bait.
He looked at his new lure.
"Guaranteed to work," he said to himself.
Max cast out his line.
"You are some kind of fisherman,"
Dad said.
Max beamed.

But fishing seemed to take forever.
Nothing happened—not even a nibble.
While Max waited, Dad caught three fish.
Max worried.
"What do you think is wrong?" he asked.
"Fishing takes time, Max," Dad said.
"But catching fish is worth the wait!"

"The package said guaranteed to work,"
Max replied.
"It will work," said Dad.
Max waited some more.
Finally, Max felt a pull on his line.
It was a very small fish.
He reeled it in, then threw it back.
"Small fry," he called after it.

Max looked at the special bait again.
He looked at the big fish
Dad had caught.
He reeled in his lure.
The feathers were droopy and wet.
The lure did not look so beautiful now.
Max put the lure where it would dry safely.
He reached for the lucky bait.
He rolled a bit of it into a ball
and baited his hook.

He cast out his line again.
Dad smiled.
Max wondered and waited.
He felt a pull.
"Look at your line!" Dad whispered.
Dad moved closer.
Max looked worried.
Max turned the crank.
The fish was heavy.

Dad helped Max reel it in.
It was a big fish—a rainbow trout.
"How big is it?" Dad asked.
Max thought a minute.
"Eight pounds?" he said.
"That is a big fish!" Dad said.
"This trout is just what my stomach wants."
"Not this one—this is for Jax,"
Max said, smiling.
"She loves rainbow trout."

Max felt a drop.
Dad felt a drop, too.
In a few minutes, it would be pouring.
"I think we should sleep under the stars
when it is not raining," Max said.
"I agree," Dad said.
"Let's head for home!"
Max smiled.

7
Raining All the Way Home

It rained all the way home.
The girls were stuck inside the house.
Jax wondered if the bait was working.
She looked out the window.
At least the seedlings in her garden
were happy.

33

The back door flew open.
Max stood at the door,
holding his prize fish.
"Look what I caught!" He beamed.
The girls screamed and squirmed.
Mom came into the kitchen.

"What is all the noise?" she asked.
"Smelly fish," Katie said.
Max plopped the fish on the table.
Katie got splashed with fishy drops.
"Look at the fish I caught!"
Max beamed.

Dad was making a nice puddle
on the kitchen floor.
"Eeeeeoooo!" the girls all screamed.
"Get that fish away from me!"
Tara yelled.

Jax reached for it.

"What a catch!" she told Max.

She carried it to the sink.

"It has got to be at least eight pounds,"
Jax said.

"Mmmmm—rainbow trout, my favorite.
You are some kind of fisherman!"

"I caught it just for you," Max said.
"You are giving it to me?"
Jax asked with surprise.
"For luck," Max said,
"and for the next time."